EASY READERS

A Beginning-to-Read Book

The Little Cookie

by Margaret Hillert

Illustrated by Donald Charles

NORWOODHOUSE🏠PRESS

DEAR CAREGIVER, The *Beginning-to-Read* series is a carefully written collection of classic readers you may remember from your own childhood. Each book features text comprised of common sight words to provide your child ample practice reading the words that appear most frequently in written text. The many additional details in the pictures enhance the story and offer the opportunity for you to help your child expand oral language and develop comprehension.

Begin by reading the story to your child, followed by letting him or her read familiar words and soon your child will be able to read the story independently. At each step of the way, be sure to praise your reader's efforts to build his or her confidence as an independent reader. Discuss the pictures and encourage your child to make connections between the story and his or her own life. At the end of the story, you will find reading activities and a word list that will help your child practice and strengthen beginning reading skills.

Above all, the most important part of the reading experience is to have fun and enjoy it!

Shannon Cannon

Shannon Cannon,
Literacy Consultant

Norwood House Press • P.O. Box 316598 • Chicago, Illinois 60631
For more information about Norwood House Press please visit our website at *www.norwoodhousepress.com* or call 866-565-2900.

LIBRARY OF CONGRESS CATALOGING-IN-PUBLICATION DATA
Hillert, Margaret.
  The little cookie : the Gingerbread boy retold / by Margaret Hillert ;
illustrated by Donald Charles.— Rev. and expanded library ed.
    p. cm. — (Beginning to read series. Fairy tales and folklore)
  Summary: A runaway gingerbread boy eludes the hungry grasp of everyone
until he meets a fox. Includes reading activities.
  ISBN-13: 978-1-59953-024-6 (library edition : alk. paper)
  ISBN-10: 1-59953-024-4 (library edition : alk. paper)
  [1. Folklore. 2. Readers.] I. Charles, Donald, ill. II. Title. III. Series.
  PZ8.1.H539Li 2006
  398.2—dc22   2005033498

See me work.
I can make something.
I can make a cookie,
a funny little cookie.

4

Look, look.
See the funny cookie.
It is little.

Oh, look.
See it go.
It can run and jump.
It can run away.

No, no, little cookie.
Come here. Come here.
I want you.

No, no.
See me go.
I can run and play.
I can run away.
You can not get me.

It is fun to run.
It is fun to play.
I can run, run, run.
I can run away.

I can go up.

I can go down.
Away, away, away.

Cookie, cookie.
Come here.
Come here to me.
I want you.

No, no.
See me go.
I can run and play.
I can run away.
You can not get me.

Look up, cookie.
Look up here.
Come to me.
I want you.

No, no.
See me go.
I can run and play.
I can run away.
You can not get me.

Look down, cookie.
Look down here.
Come into my house.
I want you.

No, no.
See me go.
I can run and play.
I can run away.
You can not get me.

17

Cookie, cookie.
See big me.
I want you.
Come here to me.

No, no.
See me go.
I can run and play.
I can run away.
You can not get me.

Come here, little cookie.
I want you.
Run, run, run.
Run here to me.

No, no.
See me go.
I can run and play.
I can run away.
You can not get me.

Oh, my.
I can not go here.
I can not go in here.

Come to me, little cookie.
I can help you.
I can go in.

One, two, three.
Here we go!

Oh, no! Oh, no!
Look at me now.
What is this?
This is not good.
No, this is not good!

READING REINFORCEMENT

The following activities support the findings of the National Reading Panel that determined the most effective components for reading instruction are: Phonemic Awareness, Phonics, Vocabulary, Fluency, and Text Comprehension.

Phonemic Awareness: The /k/ sound made with c

Oral Blending: Explain to your child that sometimes the letter **c** makes the same sound as **k**. Say the beginning and ending sounds of the following words and ask your child to listen to the sounds and say the whole word:

/k/ + at = cat	/k/ + ab = cab	/k/ + ane = cane
/k/ + ow = cow	/k/ + oat = coat	/k/ + an = can
/k/ + old = cold	/k/ + amp = camp	/k/ + ub = cub

Phonics: The letter Cc

1. Demonstrate how to form the letters **C** and **c** for your child.

2. Have your child practice writing **C** and **c** at least three times each.

3. Ask your child to point to the words in the book that start with the letter **c.**

4. Write down the following words and ask your child to circle the letter **c** in each word:

can	carry	cookie	pack	cat	come
case	rack	car	tractor	sack	cracker

Vocabulary: Verbs

1. Explain to your child that words that describe actions are called verbs.

2. Ask your child to name as many action words (verbs) as possible. Write the words on separate pieces of paper

3. Read each word to your child and ask your child to repeat it.

4. Mix the words up. Point to a word and ask your child to read it. Provide clues if your child needs them.

5. Read the following sentences to your child. Ask your child to provide an appropriate verb to complete the sentence.

   - The woman in the story _____ a cookie.
   - The cookie could _____ and _____.
   - At school, we _____ lots of books.
   - I like to _____ outside with my friends.

Fluency: Refrain

1. Reread the story to your child at least two more times while your child tracks the print by running a finger under the words as they are read. Ask your child to read the words he or she knows with you.

2. The sentences on page 9 are called a refrain because they are repeated throughout the story. Read the refrain to your child, stopping after each sentence to allow your child to echo you.

3. Help your child practice reading the entire refrain.

4. Reread the story, stopping at pages that have the refrain to let your child read it. Encourage your child to read with expression.

Text Comprehension: Discussion Time

1. Ask your child to retell the sequence of events in the story.

2. To check comprehension, ask your child the following questions:

   - What animals wanted to get the Little Cookie?
   - Why did the Little Cookie need help getting across the water?
   - Could this story really happen? Why or why not?

The Little Cookie uses the 48 words listed below.

This list can be used to practice reading the words that appear in the text. You may wish to write the words on index cards and use them to help your child build automatic word recognition. Regular practice with these words will enhance your child's fluency in reading connected text.

a	get	little	see
and	go	look	something
at	good		
away		make	the
	help	me	this
big	here	my	three
	house		to
can		no	two
come	I	not	
cookie	in	now	up
	into		
down	is	oh	want
	it	one	we
fun			what
funny	jump	play	work
		run	you

ABOUT THE AUTHOR Margaret Hillert has written over 80 books for children who are just learning to read. Her books have been translated into many different languages and over a million children throughout the world have read her books. She first started writing poetry as a child and has continued to write for children and adults throughout her life. A first grade teacher for 34 years, Margaret is now retired from teaching and lives in Michigan where she likes to write, take walks in the morning, and care for her three cats.

Photograph by Glenna Washburn

ABOUT THE ADVISER Shannon Cannon contributed the activities pages that appear in this book. Shannon serves as a literacy consultant and provides staff development to help improve reading instruction. She is a frequent presenter at educational conferences and workshops. Prior to this she worked as an elementary school teacher and as president of a curriculum publishing company.